DRABBLEDARK

AN ANTHOLOGY OF DARK DRABBLES

EDITED BY ERIC S. FOMLEY

For Cassy, my better half.

ACKNOWLEDGMENTS

I would like to specifically thank Antoinettemarie Kalmus, Edmund Schluessel, Matt Miller, Tiff Reynolds, Tianna Grosch, JT Grosch, Joseph, David, Benjamin Widmer, Software Bloke, Valeria Ballerini for their support of this project. I couldn't have done it without you. Also, a shout out belongs to Mr. Scott King for volunteering to format the anthology so that more money could go to the authors.

THE MIRROR IN THE BATHROOM

GEORGE NIKOLOPOULOS

Originally Published in Grievous Angel

Officer Jake Delonghi muttered angrily to himself, while shaving. "Another end-of-world prophecy; a mysterious invasion happening today and everyone's going to die. It's in the Potatonic Manuscripts or something. What's worse, the idiots in the Department believe it. We're working double shifts tonight. Is this pathetic or what?"

Looking at the mirror, he saw himself smiling, though he most certainly wasn't. Perplexed, he put the razor down. His reflection held it up.

"They're right about the invasion," he heard his reflection say. "In fact, we're invading you right now." Then he reached out of the mirror and cut Jake's throat.

George Nikolopoulos is a speculative fiction writer from Greece and a member of Codex Writers' Group. His stories have been published in Galaxy's Edge, Daily Science Fiction, Factor Four, Grievous Angel, Unsung Stories, Best Vegan SFF, The Year's Best Military & Adventure SF, and many more magazines and anthologies.

TRICKS FOR KIDS

JASON PLOUFFE

Wos loved Yunta. But he was still using.
Most heavily, perversely, during the child's visits.
Only the apothecary knew.
"Don't touch that!"
"Stay out of the circle!"
He didn't mean to yell. It was the cravings.
His knees ached from hours drawing on the floor.
"Just a little prick of blood for Daddy's trick."
Synapses sparked with anticipation.
He uttered the evocation perfectly.
Hurled bloodsand into the intricate circle.
Soared rushing swells of power.
A third presence entered the tiny room.
"Spin for us, Abyss Dweller."
It laughed.
Too late, Wos noticed the smudge of chalk on Yunta's tiny toes.

Jason Plouffe is a hitchhiking, comic collecting costume enthusiast who grew up beside the Indian River in Douro, Ontario, Canada. He is a founding member of Knifehammer, a spandex thrash glam outfit from Peterborough, Ontario. Nomadic by nature, Jason currently maintains a base of operations in Downtown Toronto.

TEPID TOES

C. H. WILLIAMS

They had both been so patient. Two years of holding hands on darkened streets, after the kids had gone up to bed. Stolen kisses in the shadows, their desire distressed by their deviance. Their passion came tainted with paranoia.

He left his wife and quit his job.

With a cupcake in one hand and the balloon's ribbon in the other, he cracked a wide smile and kicked open the door.

"Happy Bir--"

She smiled back at him as she swung gently from the rafters. Her bare feet were still lukewarm.

The balloon joined her body as he let it go.

Full-time mummy and author. C. H. Williams writes women's fiction but also dabbles in short stories and flash pieces for other genres.

FEASTING FOR GODS

SCOTT KING

The reflection was not Sally's, yet it moved as she did. The webbing, pus kissed tendrils, and oozing lesions made her want to look away, but she dare not.

The flames of the bathroom's antique lamp flickered. The creature blinked.

This was her chance!

Ripples ran across the mirror, as she plunged her hand into it. Nails digging, she gorged out the creature's top left eye. Like a grape, the eyeball popped in Sally's mouth. Its essences flowed in a gooey sludge, tasting sweet and bitter, like decaying tears. Immortality would be hers. When it was, the gods would die.

Scott King received his undergraduate degree in film from Towson University, and his M.F.A. from American University. Until moving to follow his wife's career, King worked as college professor teaching photography, digital arts, and writing related classes. He now works as a full time author. Learn more at: www.ScottKing.info.

THE BASEMENT

PATRICK WINTERS

It's in the basement.

It won't leave me be. I can hear it at all hours, moaning in the day and wailing at night. It's driving me crazy, scratching its fingers against the old trap-door in the kitchen floor, wanting to get out and take my life. I hate it. It scares me and I hate it.

It's scratching again, begging me to let it out.

I work up my courage and stomp on the door, shouting "Shut up! Just shut up!"

My son goes quiet again, at least for a while.

But it'll keep on trying to get out . . .

Patrick Winters is a graduate of Illinois College in Jacksonville, IL, where he earned a degree in English Literature/Creative Writing. He's been published in the likes of Sanitarium Magazine, Deadman's Tome, and Trysts of Fate. A full list of his previous publications may be found at his author's site: http://wintersauthor.azurewebsites.net/Pages/Previous%20Publications.

THE CHOICE

BART VAN GOETHEM

They say in space no one can hear you scream. They are wrong. I screamed and the Am'ent came and they took me to their home. A world that begins where pain ends. They rebuilt me, slowly, gruelingly, literally, until I was one of them. So just remember, when you're floating around in the black nothingness, with the oxygen levels nearing the red mark inevitably and you are about to clutch with both hands your last straw that is a cry for help, you have a choice: choke in silence or be reborn in agony. I wish I had known.

Bart Van Goethem. Micro and flash fiction writer. Drummer. Addict (Real Racing 3). His goal is to play his way through life. So far, so good. Follow him @bartvangoethem.

CHILL

ALEX SHVARTSMAN

This old book had some seriously heavy stuff, man. Potion recipes, curses and spells; you know, the works. It even explained how to summon a demon and make it grant you a single wish. Totally radical, you dig? I followed the instructions and there it was, an ugly little critter screaming its head off inside the pentagram.

"Dude, like, chill," I told it. The beastie quit screaming, laughed and then disappeared. I tried summoning it again, but no luck.

It's been getting a little colder every day since then. Yesterday it snowed in LA, in June! I'm beginning to worry.

Alex Shvartsman is a writer, translator, and anthologist from Brooklyn, NY. Over 100 of his short stories have appeared in Nature, Analog, Strange Horizons, and many other magazines and anthologies. His website is www.alexshvartsman.com.

WALKERS

SHAUN AVERY

Suckers.

Out walking.

I hacked into their precious step-counting watches, can see when they're using them. Got their addresses, too, going to rob them all. Starting with the nearest.

Soon I'm standing at the door, jimmying knife in hand.

But the door's already open.

Suckers, I think, striding inside.

But I get a big shock.

See a sweat-covered woman there, walking around the living room.

She sees my knife, obviously misunderstands my intentions, screams.

Her husband runs down the stairs, holding a gun.

Which fires.

Sucker.

It never occurred to me they could be getting their steps inside the house.

Shaun Avery's work appears in many anthologies and magazines. He is a fan of walking but not the gym, having found it, the one time he went, to be nothing like in the video for Take That's It Only Takes a Minute. Perhaps he just found the wrong gym.

AN UNDENIABLE TRUTH

NORA WESTON

Knock, knock…

"Who's there?" asked Seth.

"Me," answered the visitor. "Or *you*. Depends which side of the door you're on."

"What?" Seth looked through the peep hole. No one. "Freaking kids…"

Twelve minutes died.

Knock, knock…

"Oh, come on!" Annoyed, Seth did not want to stop working on his latest gem, a miniature, yellow 1970 Dodge Challenger.

Pounding on the door became excessive.

Seth tossed the glue, rushed to open the door. "Huh? *What the…*"

"Greetings, MDX21V4," said his duplicate. "You've expired. Pardon my disappearance. Phone call ."

"No way," said Seth in shock.

"Well, nothing lasts forever," said MDX21V5.

Nora Weston is a Michigan based writer/artist. Her publishing credits include novels, anthologies, plus fiction and poetry in various magazines, including; Hoboeye, The Harrow, Eye to the Telescope, Calliope on the Web, Bete Noire, and NewMyths.com. Recent work has been published by Star*Line, Ramingo's Porch, and Bull & Cross.

SECRET RENDEZVOUS

MICHAEL BALLETTI

I can't believe I'm doing this! The idea popped into my head the first time you started talking to me at the train station. I must've looked like prey to your wolfish eyes. All it took was a few coy smiles to get you going about your unhappy marriage. And your eyes nearly bulged when I finally invited you out for a drink. Yes, that's when I slipped you the toxin. It paralyzes but doesn't kill. That's my job. I won't lie—you'll feel everything. Don't worry, this will stay between you and me. Your wife won't know a thing.

Michael Balletti lives in New Jersey. His work has appeared in Theme of Absence, 200 CCs, The Last Line and Sanitarium Magazine, among others.

BOGEYMAN

PATRICK WINTERS

I've been forgotten.

Once, I was great and terrible. The eye to all of little Sarah's storming fears. I would scratch my finger against the floorboards, or chuckle in my dark way, and she would cower under the covers. And if ever I reared up to reveal my horrible self, she would scream.

But Sarah no longer screams. She has grown accustomed to staying quiet, and I've since withered, left to the dusty dark beneath her mattress.

Because she no longer fears what's under her bed; she fears the bedroom door. She fears when it will open.

She fears him.

Patrick Winters is a graduate of Illinois College in Jacksonville, IL, where he earned a degree in English Literature/Creative Writing. He's been published in the likes of Sanitarium Magazine, Deadman's Tome, and Trysts of Fate. A full list of his previous publications may be found at his author's site: http://wintersauthor.azurewebsites.net/Pages/Previous%20Publications.

THE WOODS BEHIND THE HOUSE

TAMLYN DREAVER

My mother died when I was seven. I watched it happen.

The most horrific death of the century, the tabloids said. Blood coated the walls and dripped from the ceiling. Blood covered me. An officer joked – out of my hearing – that they'd be finding pieces of my mother for years to come.

A monster, they said, and others said impossible.

It was a monster. It came from the woods behind the house.

They said there was nothing I could have done. They were wrong. There was something, and I did it.

I laid the bait. I invited the monster in.

Tamlyn Dreaver grew up in rural Western Australia, spent eight years in Melbourne, and is now back in Perth. She's never had a secret basement or a dragon nesting in the backyard so she writes stories about them instead.

She can be found at www.tamlyndreaver.com and tweeting at @tamlyn_-dreaver.

XI'S BEAST

RIVER RIVERS

A Sphinxling lay at her feet. It's two heads on a single body reached out curiously. Both a kitten and a dog, it's four eyes had just opened.

Weakness clung to Xi like a nasty skin infection.

She let down her cloak as the mouthless assassin spoke into darkness, "You have killed men, women, and children. Yet, blood has never touched your lips." The Teacher removed a dagger from its sheath for her to take. "I respect the decision. Your culture demands it. Though, we Reapers must slay beast and man alike."

"I understand, Master." She whispered as the beast whimpered.

River Rivers is a writer lost in the Cascadian mountain lands of Oregon. He spends his time with his two adopted Pitbulls, Gemma and Murphy. Somehow in between their chaos, he finds a time for work and fiction. His most recent work is currently featured on Literally Stories, Who Writes Short Shorts, and TallTaleTv in May.

BODY JEWELRY

DANIELLE DELISLE

Spinal cords are ethereal. Beautiful. Their opalescent sheen reflects all the colors of the rainbow as you turn them in the light. This hidden beauty deep inside us longs to shine. Did you know round molds can be found at most hobby stores, and spinal cords are easy to preserve if you use the right epoxy? The thin organ looks amazing, even on the daintiest of wrists. A quick, machine polish completes each unique masterpiece. I get compliments from strangers all the time, and when anyone asks me where I got my bracelet, I show them. I made hundreds. Look.

Danielle DeLisle writes horror, fantasy, and science fiction. She can be found online at www.danielledelisle.com.

CONFESSION

ROBERT DAWSON

Father Blaire sat silently in the booth. A mother might steal to feed her children, a soldier kill to protect the innocent, but the seal of the confessional had no exceptions, even to save life.

Every few weeks, a young man vanished; it was all over the newspapers. Days later, the bodies reappeared: bound, slashed, and mutilated. Everybody knew that, too.

Each time, while the police searched and hope ebbed, the hoarse-voiced stranger attended Confession, describing horrors corroborated later by the mute testimony of the bodies. And only Father Blaire knew that.

He gripped the Glock with sweating hands, waiting.

———————

Robert Dawson teaches mathematics. In between times, he writes, cycles, hikes, and fences. His stories have appeared in Nature Futures, AE, Speck Lit,and numerous other periodicals and anthologies. He is an alumnus of the Viable Paradise and Sage Hill writing workshops.

PRISONER

ALYSON FAYE

Your skin is growing paler every day. No sun reaches you down here. Daily we gather to pray at your bedside, holding our shields in gloved hands. We dare not touch you.

'Forgive us,' we whisper.

Your eyes tell us that will never happen.

When we found you, you were dying. We fed you our finest kids.

Now the chains barely restrain you.

We fear you, but we need you.

Outside the village clock strikes thirteen. Time has missed a beat.

It is coming. The Devourer.

We shall unleash you, our weapon, our savior.

Let the dragons roam once more.

Alyson lives in West Yorkshire, UK, where she writes her noir tales of horror in between teaching classes, editing, being a mum, and looking after 4 rescue animals. She loves old movies, reading, crafting, swimming and singing. Her blog is at www.alysonfayewordpress.wordpress.com.

WE ARE THE GLITTEREANS

STEPHEN D. ROGERS

We were drawn inside the building by the flashing lights. We entered through cracks and closing doors, and then we were trapped.

Doomed by our desires.

So many I saw killed. So very, very many. They flew to exhaustion while chasing the dancing sparkles, or they drowned in pools of glowing effervescence. So very, very many.

The room pulsing so loudly we couldn't even hear each other scream.

My wing damaged in a midair collision left me panting on the sidelines as the slaughter continued until the lights finally died.

The building went dark.

Those of us remaining staggered free.

Stephen D. Rogers is the author of more than 800 shorter works. His website, www.StephenDRogers.com, includes a list of new and upcoming titles as well as other timely information.

POOR NATHAN

PATRICK WINTERS

It was an accident. Her poor Nathan had just reached the top of the stairs. Then he was falling. She saw the whole thing from their bedroom door. He was coming up to bed, but his bad leg—he was so unsteady these days. She'd talked about getting one of those motorized chairs installed, but Nathan wouldn't have it. He was so stubborn.

When she'd got to the bottom of the stairs, it was already too late.

Her poor, poor Nathan.

Yes, that's what Joan would tell authorities when they came.

But right now, her husband was coming up the stairs.

Patrick Winters is a graduate of Illinois College in Jacksonville, IL, where he earned a degree in English Literature/Creative Writing. He's been published in the likes of Sanitarium Magazine, Deadman's Tome, and Trysts of Fate. A full list of his previous publications may be found at his author's site: http://wintersauthor.azurewebsites.net/Pages/Previous%20Publications.

THERE'LL ALWAYS BE TEARS

KAREN HESLOP

"Why don't you just cry?" he asks.

Ijela glares, fire blazing where he wishes to see tears.

"How would tears fix this?"

A light chuckle hiccups from his blistered lips.

"You mean the air or what's left of my pretty face?"

She marvels at his sense of humor while his insides disintegrate. She reaches for his hand and her shoulders slump. Just like his legs, the putrefying skin of his palms has fused.

"Why'd you take the mask off, Jax?"

"Far from…the last nuclear blast," he whispers.

Blood streams from the corner of his lips.

Tears slip unto her cheeks.

Karen Heslop writes from Kingston, Jamaica. Her stories have been published or are upcoming in Grievous Angel, Speculative 66, The Future Fire and 4StarStories among others. She tweets @kheslopwrites.

BROKEN

BRANDON BARROWS

Kira leaned against the bathroom sink, carefully avoiding the mirror's gaze, knowing what she'd see. The unwashed hair, puffy eyes and cracked lips she could handle, could control, if inclined.

It was the smile she feared. It didn't belong to her, never appeared on her face, but always beamed from her mirror.

Steeling herself, she glanced at the reflection: her own ravaged face grinned maliciously back, just as it had for months.

Her frustrated fist shot towards the mirror, shattering it.

Wincing, she chanced another look and her heart sank. Even without the mirror, that evil smile remained.

Kira screamed.

Brandon Barrows is the award-nominated author of the occult-noir novel THIS ROUGH OLD WORLD as well as over fifty published stories, selected of which have been collected into the books THE ALTAR IN THE HILLS and THE CASTLE-TOWN TRAGEDY. Find more at www.brandonbarrows-comics.com and on Twitter @BrandonBarrows.

DIRGE

MELANIE NOELL BERNARD

Wind whispered through the trees, forcing barren branches to dance to a macabre tune. A tune, heard only by the dead.

But she was neither dead nor dying. She lived, breathed, felt. Her kind was not allowed, yet she strode forward as if in a trance, following the dangerous melody.

Disturbed by her presence, the wind swelled. It twisted the notes to tear at her hair and claw at her dress. She spun round, trying to catch every lilt and chord, but so caught up was she, that all else was forgotten. For this was a place of the dead.

Melanie Noell Bernard hails from the Midwest. Surrounded by endless fog and bitter winter nights, she quickly fell in love with the dark. Combine that with a knack for the gritty, the disturbing, and the creepy, you have the beginnings of a horror writer.

LOST LIFE

ETHAN HEDMAN

The store's glass doors slide open. Air bursts from overhead fans. Accumulated dust swirls towards the outside world.

"Welcome," calls a disembodied voice. "Please let us know if you need anything."

Officer 10642 ignores the greeting. It walks to the center of the store and initiates Scanning Protocol 1. High-pitched pings emit from its swiveling head to analyze a full echolocation profile of its surroundings.

No biological activity detected.

The Officer reports its findings. Aerial Surveillance Unit 8311 transmits the next location.

The search has gone on for months. The Officer's probability program suggests there is nothing to be found.

Ethan Hedman conjures ideas, writes words, and shares stories. His full bibliography can be found on EthanHedman.com.

PRECIOUS THINGS

MICHELLE ANN KING

I found it in the woods. It didn't belong to anyone, so I took it home. It was pretty.

My wife didn't like it. She said a lot of stupid stuff about it. But people get sick sometimes, shit goes wrong. That's just how life is.

And I got better, anyway. I'm fine now.

She said I had to get rid of it, but I couldn't bear to just throw it away. So I buried it under the house.

I might not be able to look at it any more, but I know that it's there. And it's still pretty.

Michelle Ann King was born in East London and now lives in Essex. Her stories have appeared in over seventy different venues, including Interzone, Strange Horizons, and Black Static. See www.transientcactus.co.uk for links to her published works.

SILICON TWINS

RUSSELL HEMMELL

"I'm better."

"No, you're just prettier."

The mainframe's AI and I discuss every day - fighting, pleading, negotiating, and finally agreeing on letting each other be, for we don't have a choice.

Kara is captive into a silicon universe, with an all-powerful, artificial brain and no body. When she wants to feel, she has to use mine.

Me? I'm free to walk away and roam the streets, but without her it's not life, it's survival.

Kara gives me access to worlds without borders, aliens shores and galaxies of light, where blinking is time-travel and a dream is a never-ending goodbye.

Russell Hemmell is a statistician and social scientist from the U.K, passionate about astrophysics and speculative fiction. Recent/forthcoming publications in Aurealis, New Myths, Not One of Us, and others. Find her online at her blog earthianhivemind.net and on Twitter @SPBianchini.

THE BLACKBIRD KING

WENDY NIKEL

Originally Published in SpeckLit

Only a mad king would demand a pie of blackbirds. He ordered twenty-four birds be slaughtered, diced, and cooked for the crime of robbing the royal fruit trees. Yet when the baker presented the fragrant dish, the crust held only six. Six whirring, clanking clockwork crows with wispy feathers of gold, secretly constructed by the kingdom's finest tinkerers deep in the rebels' quarters.

His knife sliced the pie, meeting metal rather than meat.

The crows burst forth, brandishing their needle-sharp claws as weapons, their tiny beaks as spears.

The king fell, clutching his heart, in a heap of bloodstained feathers.

Wendy Nikel's fiction has appeared in Fantastic Stories of the Imagination, Daily Science Fiction, Nature: Futures, and elsewhere.

THE LADY ON THE BUS

BRENDA ANDERSON

The lady on the bus bent over her empty stroller and whispered something into its depths. When she alighted from the bus, on an impulse, so did I.

The road led to the cemetery, and a grave. Here she stopped and undid the strap.

"That was nice, Mary, wasn't it?" She turned and patted the headstone. "We're back again, Michelle. Your turn, now."

As she collapsed the stroller, she noticed me.

"Conjoined twins, you see. They're so needy." She gave a radiant smile. "I take them for a walk separately. It's so much better this way, don't you think? Fairer?"

Brenda Anderson's fiction has appeared in various places including Daily Science Fiction and Flash Fiction Online. She lives in Adelaide, South Australia, and tweets irregularly @CinnamonShops.

SHE'D EXPECTED TO SEE SOME BLOOD

STEVE CAMPBELL

Originally Published in Sick Lit Magazine

She pries out one of its eyeballs with the tip of a screwdriver and rolls it around between her fingers. She'd expected to see some blood. Shrugging, she starts ripping off its slutty clothes until the banging door breaks her concentration.

"Jenniieee!" The door rattles in the frame. "Jenny. Open the door."

She scrapes up the clothes and bundles it under the bed, keeping the scissors held tightly behind her back as she opens the door.

"Where's my Sindy?!" Her sister shoves her way into the bedroom. "I'm telling Mom!"

"Telling Mom what?" Jenny asks, closing the door behind them.

Steve Campbell has short fiction published in places such as Sick Lit Magazine, formercactus, Twisted Sister Lit Mag, Occulum and MoonPark Review, and on his website standondog.com. He somehow finds time to manage EllipsisZine.com. You can follow him on twitter here: @standondog.

GALA DOWN

SARA CODAIR

Silence is bliss after hours of false politicking.

A man can only tolerate so much entitled bigotry.

The presidential candidate slumps in his cake, like the venom of his words poisoned it. His wife's head lolls; blood streams from her nose, staining her silky gown.

Minutes ago, she fluttered with champagne in hand, praising the new manager for his opulent venue choice.

Now, only the old manager, a tall man in a gasmask, wanders through the corpses. He worked hard, carrying countless politicians to The Whitehouse regardless of their policies.

This was different.

He couldn't hand power to these monsters.

Sara Codair lives in a world of words where writing is like breathing. They live with a cat, Goose, who "edits" their work by deleting entire pages. Their short stories appear in Unnerving Magazine, Alternative Truths, and Helios Quarterly. Find Sara online at https://saracodair.com/ or @shatteredsmooth.

NEXT TIME LOOK IN THE CABBAGE PATCH

JOHN H. DROMEY

Originally Published in Daily Frights 2012: 366 Days of Dark Flash Fiction

"What's the matter with her?" a wide-eyed youngster asked as a woman with a bulging midsection was rushed into the emergency room.

"She swallowed a watermelon seed," a nurse said.

The inquisitive boy's father took umbrage. "How dare you lie to my child? You should simply have told him she's pregnant."

"I wasn't lying," the nurse said. "The seed she swallowed was genetically altered."

The ER doctor staggered into the waiting room, gasping for air and trying desperately to remove the pulsating green umbilical cord that was coiled tightly around his neck and slowly squeezing the life out of him.

———

John H. Dromey enjoys reading—mysteries especially—and writing in a variety of genres. He's had short fiction published in Alfred Hitchcock's Mystery Magazine, Crimson Streets, Stupefying Stories Showcase, and elsewhere, as well as in a number of anthologies, including Chilling Horror Short Stories (Flame Tree Publishing, 2015).

29

THE WAXING OF A BLOOD MOON

HAMILTON KHOL

Marquardt tasted the alpha's scent on the wind. The elders had been right. Each night for a month they bayed of the coming blood moon. And now red marred the sky.

The goddess who called them to change, the night pearl, was painted in fire making all equal while she burned. Bone snapped, sinew stretched, and skin tore as his wolf's mane grew.

The broken and misshaped maw of the werewolf could not grin. But inside the beast, Marquardt's smile promised blood and retribution. His howl raged up to the goddess, vengeful and fierce.

The alpha's scent turned to fear.

Hamilton Kohl spends his days chained to an office cubicle and writing whenever the corporate alpha's aren't looking. At night he's allowed a brief reprieve to spend time with his wife and children where they live just outside of Toronto, Canada.

ALL YOU LOVE IS NEED

KARL LYKKEN

"My mother told me a boy would only love the girl he needs," Lorelei said, setting down the mallet. "That's why I tutored you, until you got the hang of math and didn't need me anymore. So I tried to be your girl Friday, but there were prettier girls you let wait on you. You had their love; you didn't need mine. But where are those girls now?"

Lorelei pulled the ice pick out from Billy's eye, gently wiping up the drips of blood. "Now that your lobotomy is complete, you'll need care forever. You'll need me forever, my love."

Karl Lykken writes both stories and software in Texas. His dark fiction has appeared in Theme of Absence, Feed Your Monster, and 9Tales at the World's End No. 4.

LESSON LEARNED

HOLLY SCHOFIELD

Originally Published in SpeckLit

The robots awoke Kyle and the thousand other students from stasis. A dusty orange planet loomed in the viewport. Kyle grinned.

A new world! Soon they would start terraforming it. What a terrific undergrad course!

The ship landed and the lock cycled open before any of the students had their suits on. Robots pushed them all out, against their protests. They would all asphyxiate in minutes. Kyle fell to his knees on the powdery alien soil.

"Help!"

A robot, unloading oxygen-producing machinery, glanced where Kyle lay gasping. "Lesson Number One: The easiest way to terraform is to use organic fertilizer."

Holly Schofield's stories have appeared in Analog, Lightspeed, Escape Pod, and many other publications throughout the world. You can find her at hollyschofield.wordpress.com.

TINY DOOR

DAVID AFSHARIRAD

Originally Published in SpeckLit

While cleaning out the basement in my house, I find a tiny door, set into the far back wall. The door is a perfect replica of the one that is set into the front of my house.

I open it. Inside is a copy of my living room, exact in every detail. It is while contemplating this odd occurrence that I see him.

Another me. A tiny me.

I dash up the basement steps and throw myself face-down on the couch, terrified.

I feel the breeze on my neck.

I look up to see the eye that fills my doorway.

––––––––––

David Afsharirad is the editor of The Year's Best Military and Adventure SF series, from Baen Books. His short stories and nonfiction have appeared in various magazines and journals. He lives in Austin, TX.

I DO

P. R. O'LEARY

The eternal love we pledged at the altar was a vow I had fully meant to keep. But now, I am finding it very difficult. Standing at her grave, my hands holding flowers for her headstone, I watch as her tattered corpse rises from the earth. Her pale dirty hands outstretch and reach towards me. Her bony feet shuffle forward. A guttural groan comes from her torn throat and her teeth click together in anticipation of flesh. Still, I remember my vows. When my wife's arms reach out to grab at my neck, I move forward for one last embrace.

P. R. O'Leary writes and make films so someday he won't have to work in a cubicle. In between these spurts of creativity he enjoys running long distances and attending film festivals. You can find his work at www.PROleary.com and you can find him at his geodesic dome in NJ.

AN INEFFABLE SITUATION

JOHN H. DROMEY

Originally Published in Sirens Call eZine #32 Slash and Hack

Screaming loudly, Leon awoke in a hospital.

A hazmat-suited orderly approached the patient's bed and asked in a voice muffled by an opaque visor, "What's the matter?"

Leon answered, "In a nightmare, I dreamed Earth lost an intergalactic conflict with cannibalistic invaders from Grawlix... the Cussing Planet. They were trying to fatten me up for slaughter."

"What a crock of freaking, blankety-blank, steaming bleep!" the orderly mumbled.

A second attendant approached carrying a carving knife. Unlike his disguised-as-a-human colleague, this clumsy creature was not wearing his shapeshifting camo suit. He stubbed a tentacle, and said, "#@%^! *$<!"

Leon resumed screaming.

John H. Dromey enjoys reading—mysteries especially—and writing in a variety of genres. He's had short fiction published in Alfred Hitchcock's Mystery Magazine, Crimson Streets, Stupefying Stories Showcase, and elsewhere, as well as in a number of anthologies, including Chilling Horror Short Stories (Flame Tree Publishing, 2015).

THE CANDY FACTORY

NICO BELL

It started as a dare. Twenty bucks to last one hour inside the deserted candy factory. I ignored the knot in my throat, stepped inside, eyed the draping cobwebs and reconsidered. But defeat meant heckling from my friends.

No thanks.

A soft whistling melody startled my nerves as I turned toward the music.

A man stepped into the hall.

I gasped as I stared into his lemon sour eyes. Caramel replaced his skin and dripped to the floor. He froze.

A bang echoed from above.

The man winced, opened his Twizzler lips, uttered a single word.

"Run."

Nico Bell writes dark fiction, horror and science fiction. She can be found on twitter @nicobellfiction.com or facebook at www.facebook.com/nicobellfiction.

REPAST

AM KALMUS

Dappled sunlight left spots of shadow shifting across a tiny woodland meadow. A family of rabbits languidly hopped about, moving from sprout to sprout enjoying an early spring snack. At the edge of the heath, amidst the evergreen scrub, verdant scales glinted in the errant beams of light. The crack of a twig sent velveteen ears swiveling, but the silence and serenity of the wood soothed away agitation, and the rabbits returned to their feasting. Shrouded in shadow, under the cover of ferns, a wedge-shaped head emerged. An inhaled breath, a puff of smoke, and a hearty lunch was served.

AM Kalmus is a Science Fiction/Fantasy author living in Helotes, TX with two Siberian cats, a crazy Australian Cattle Dog, her son, and her loving husband. To keep up with Antoinettemarie's accelerating career please visit www.amkalmus.com.

FERALIZATION

JAMES EBERSOLE

When the baby arrived, we kept the dog outside. The arrangement worked well at first, until the night we heard barking over the baby monitor. I ran into the nursery to discover our child outside its crib, giggling and finger-painting dog's blood on the walls.

We buried the dog in the woods out back.

The years passed.

Our child grew, but never learned to communicate beyond whimpers and quizzical stares.

Sometimes, in moments of respite, smoking cigarettes on the back porch, I hear an infant wailing beyond the dark wall of trees, the sound distant, as if muffled by dirt.

James Ebersole's work has appeared in such places as The Horror Writers Association Poetry Showcase, Folk Horror Revival: Corpse Roads, Richmond Macabre, Broken Worlds, and The Mammoth Book of Halloween Stories (forthcoming). He lives in Northern Virginia and holds an MA in creative writing from Edinburgh Napier University.

THE THING IN THE WALLS

DOUGLAS PRINCE

The mouse ran along the wall cavity, whiskers twitching. Eyes bright, it
scurried forward leaving tiny footprints in its wake.

It stopped.

A shadow blocked the narrow passage, looming. Fear, rage, and
sweat hung
heavy on the stagnant air.

"Ugh!"

It exploded, a fist detaching from the darkness, missing the rodent by
inches. The mouse fled as the shadow wailed its loss.

The boy squatted in the dark, face streaked with tears. One hand rested on
the floor, the other pointed skyward, handcuffed to a sturdy pipe.

Tears rolled down his cheeks, leaving dark flowers to blossom in the dust.

Douglas Prince is a 28-year-old writer of horror and other dark fiction. Born
in Melrose, Scotland, he now lives on the Wirral peninsula, in Merseyside,
where he writes stories and reads more books than can possibly be good
for him.

EARTH ANGEL

F. E. CLARK

Here lies the Earth Angel. She's just sleeping—so the legend goes. Tread carefully around the half buried form of the woman who stopped when the sorrows of world became too much. It's said her last memory was of being so unspeakably tired that she longed to lie down on the ground where she stood. She imagined grass tangling up through her hair, mushrooms growing in her soft belly—she imagined becoming rooted, steady again. That's when she closed her eyes. Some say she will wake when peace comes, others believe that she will awake and bring it with her.

F. E. Clark lives in Scotland. She writes and paints. A Pushcart and Best of the Net nominee, read her words at: Molotov Cocktail Literary Magazine, Poems for All, Occulum, Moonchild Magazine, Ink In Thirds, Poems for All, Folded Word, Ellipsis Zine, Luna Luna Magazine, and The Wild Hunt.

Website: www.feclarkart.com | Twitter: @feclarkart

AUTUMN LEAVES

DAVID BERNARD

I love everything about autumn. But my favorite part is the falling leaves that make the ground a mosaic of color. I spent the afternoon raking leaves, creating piles. Now I relax inside, waiting for dinner.

I heard the kids leaving school. My yard is a shortcut and they always stop to jump in the leaves. I really only do it for the children.

I heard the laughter turned to screams. The continued shrieking told me one of them had jumped into the pile where I hid the bear trap.

I stood up. It's time to see what's for dinner.

David Bernard is a native New Englander who lives in South Florida, albeit under protest. His previous works include short stories in anthologies such as Snowbound with Zombies (Post Mortem Press), Legacy of the Reanimator (Chaosium), and The Shadow over Deathlehem (Grinning Skull Press).

THE LIGHT

EDWARD ASHTON

I squeeze my eyes shut in the coal-black dark, and shiver as her nightmare-long arms wrap around me. Her skin is smooth and dry and fever-hot, her breath a soft hiss in my ear.

"You're sure?"

I nod.

Soft lips brush my shoulder. I shiver again as her fangs break the skin. The venom burns. She holds me as I shudder, then eases me to the floor as the euphoria hits.

"I love you," I whisper.

"I know," she says softly, from far, far away.

Her hand strokes my forehead.

Her tear strikes my cheek.

The light…

Edward Ashton is the author of the novels Three Days in April and The End of Ordinary. His short fiction has appeared in venues ranging from Flash Fiction Online and Fireside to the newsletter of an Italian sausage company. You can find him online at edwardashton.com.

TENEBRIS BOREALIS

DENNIS MOMBAUER

"Where is everyone?" Ayako and Sulawak exited the car. The forest shrouded the camp in shadow and blocked out the sky. A generator hummed, cables snaked between bright lamps. No bodies.

"Look!" Darkness swallowed the road. It washed against the lamps, burst bulbs, streamed in black rivers over the forest floor.

"Run!" They sprinted toward the car, their flashlights barely clearing a path. Inky currents flooded around them. Ayako jumped in the driver's seat.

Sulawak's flashlight flickered. The darkness surged. Ayako stepped on the gas but caught a glimpse of something pale that snatched Sulawak, a nightmarish wind: the wendigo.

Dennis Mombauer currently lives in Colombo as a freelance writer of fiction, textual experiments, reviews, & essays on climate change & education. Co-publisher of "Die Novelle – Magazine for Experimentalism". Publications in various small- to medium-sized magazines & anthologies. German novel publication "Das Maskenhandwerk" (The Mask Trade).

Homepage: www.dennismombauer.com
Facebook: www.facebook.com/DMombauer

RANGER NED COMES TO SAVE THE DAY

GARY CUBA

"Ranger Ned! You're just in time!"

Tess struggled against the ropes that bound her to the railroad tracks. The horn of the 2:16 to Calgary blared in the near distance.

Ned dismounted from his horse and crouched by Tess. "Hang on. I'll save you." He studied the knots, then tried to loosen them.

"Hurry, Ned!"

"Never was much good with knots, Tess."

"Then cut them with your knife!"

"Lost it somewhere up near Greenville."

Tess groaned. "Then shoot them free!"

"No bullets. Used 'em all up."

"You useless bast--"

Ned stepped back gingerly just before the train roared past.

Gary Cuba lives in the sticks of South Carolina. His short fiction has previously appeared in more than 100 magazines and anthologies, including Baen's Universe, Daily SF, and Nature Futures. Visit http://thefoggiestnotion.com to learn more about him and to find links to some of his other published fiction.

THE BASEMENT

EDWARD PALUMBO

The basement is cold and shadowed. The boiler heaves to break the silence and the sound chills me even more. What kind of man attacks his own mother, this kind, this man, I hear her above, tinkering in the kitchen, as if with knives, as if she is planning an experiment or a

punishment. She is not alone, not always, a neighbor visits to socialize or complain about my

screams, now and then. Soon comes the darkness, my dearest friend, my only friend. The

basement is cold, the rats scratch the timber, seeking entry. One more, one less, what matter?

Edward Palumbo is a graduate of the University of Rhode Island (1982). His fiction, poems, shorts, and journalism have appeared in numerous periodicals, journals, e-journals and anthologies including Rough Places Plain, Flush Fiction, Tertulia Magazine, Epiphany, The Poet's Page, Reader's Digest, Baseball Bard and Mystery Weekly. Ed is a prize-winning poet and playwright. Ed's literary credo is: if you fall off the horse, get right back on the bicycle.

PUSHING FORWARD

STUART CONOVER

Another band of goblins was closing in on them.

Leasep brandished her clan's pollaxe.

The obsidian blade absorbing the moonlight.

Forged deep within the mountains her people had to abandon, it hungered for the blood of her enemies.

These raids were growing more frequent as her people traveled further south.

The goblins emerged and screamed as they charged.

The dwarves were ready for them.

Ancient axes and maces made short work of these would be attackers.

As the battle drew to a close, Leasep whispered a prayer to their Gods.

They would find a new home soon.

They had to.

Stuart Conover is a father, husband, rescue dog owner, horror author, blogger, journalist, horror enthusiast, comic book geek, science fiction junkie, IT professional, and editor of The Horror Tree. With all of that to cram in on a daily basis, we have no idea if or when he sleeps!

THE HATBOX

CRAIG FAUSTUS BUCK

I happened to be the passenger who noticed the blood dripping from the suitcase on the train's overhead rack. The conductor opened the quaintly flowered case. The girl had been only nineteen or twenty. She was small, maybe ninety pounds if her head had been attached. But it wasn't there.

The conductor looked at me. Did they think I was responsible for the decapitated girl? I felt awkward, to say the least, and nauseated.

I averted my eyes and my gaze fell on a hatbox below the seat. A chill slid down my spine. The hatbox, too, was quaintly flowered.

Author-screenwriter Craig Faustus Buck's writing has won or been nominated for numerous crime fiction awards. His novel, Go Down Hard, a noir romp, was published by Brash Books. The sequel, Go Down Screaming, is coming out whenever he writes his way out of the second act.

THE EBBING TIDE CALLS

DANIEL PIETERSEN

Svensson lies in his bed, a berth the old shipmaster has rarely left in the past few years. He watches as the accusatory finger of the lighthouse sweeps across the harbor, in through the bottleglass window and onto the long, blank wall. Each pulse shines a zoetrope puppet-show onto the whitewashed brick.

An empty room. Darkness. The door, still closed, swings its shadow-self into the room. Darkness. A woman, his wife, crosses the threshold. Darkness. Halfway across the room, her features blurred as if underwater. Darkness. Seawater drips from her hair, her out-stretched hands, as she stands above him. Darkness.

Daniel Pietersen writes weird fiction and horror philosophy. He's a contributor to Hippocampus Press' Dead Reckonings journal and his essay on the limit experience in The Hellbound Heart will be published in the imminent second volume of Thinking Horror. He lives in Edinburgh, Scotland, with his wife and dog.

DARK GODDESS

JONATHAN FICKE

From the first moment that my dark goddess slid her tendrils into my blood, I was hers. She caressed my mind. Her fingers were a salve to my pain. Her presence satisfied my hunger and slaked my thirst. Memories of family and friends faded beneath her sinuous touch. They called out to me, desperate and distant. I saw the envy in their eyes. They would purge the goddess from my veins, steal her comfort from my mind. If I went with them, she would claw at my mind until I returned to her. I'd rather die than endure her absence.

Jonathan Ficke lives outside of Milwaukee with his beautiful wife. His fiction has appeared in "Writers of the Future, Vol. 34" and "Tales of Ruma," and he muses online at jonficke.com and tweets (mostly about writing, basketball, and woodworking) @jonficke.

AMONGST MARBLE AND THE DEAD

B.B. BLAZKOWICZ

As we descended into the abandoned cemetery's derelict crypt they told me to take the lead. I was growing accustomed to it.

"When did you find this place?" they asked.

"For awhile, I was just waiting for a rainy day to bring you all ."

The moment the stairs ended, the marble door slid shut. I calmly reached into my coffin and retrieved a centuries old hand-axe before turning back to them. They beheld my true ghastly visage in shock and silence.

I wryly responded to their terror:

"Philosophy's not the only way to open someone's mind."

B.B. Blazkowicz is a horror fiction writer currently tied to a chair in an Antarctic research facility. A bearded man who smells of Scotch says one of us is assimilated. If you are reading this please send me transportation to your densest population centers.

RETRIBUTION

STELLA TURNER

Tom thought it was hilarious to buy a garden gnome for a flat with no garden. Sadie thought he was an idiot standing the gnome on the bedroom windowsill. Watching them closely it needed to bide it's time. The duo lay across the bed, bodies riddled with bullets, blood smeared walls, the quilt no longer pristine white, the bedroom a crime scene. Inspector Brown was mystified no sign of a break in, no motive. The gnome spooked him, carrying a machine gun, wearing a bandolier; he'd never seen a garden gnome like that before, it should be in a garden.

Stella Turner was 'sent to Coventry', England at birth, loves the ring road, the two cathedrals and all its history. Published in several anthologies and hopes to write a best-seller which may or may not get published. She just needs to write a few more words than her usual Flashes and Drabbles.

SUICIDE HOTLINE

ELIZABETH DEARBORN

Death would release her, but suicide was wrong. With one faint wish to live, she dialed the number.

"Suicide Hotline!"

"I'm in terrible pain. Bone cancer. You can't imagine – "

"We're not in. Leave a message after the tone."

"AAAAHHHHhhhh," she screamed as she jumped.

One down!

"Suicide Hotline!"

"My wife left me. I'm gonna shoot myself."

"Sorry, we're not in. Leave your name – " Lucifer said.

BANG!

Like I care!

"Suicide Hotline!"

"I got wasted, man. I ran over some little kid – hello?"

You don't need any help from me.

Lucifer left the caller babbling into the phone and walked away.

Elizabeth Dearborn writes short fiction and computer code. She lives near the Canadian border.

ENCHANTED LEFTOVERS

JOHN H. DROMEY

Originally Published in One Star Reviews of the Afterlife: Alternate Hilarities 5

On short notice, the palace chef was commanded by royal decree to prepare a dainty dish to set before the king's daughter. With no time for shopping, he scrambled to find suitable ingredients on the castle grounds. Since he'd already done something from the air for her father—four and twenty blackbirds—the chef decided to go with something from the water: cuisses de grenouille.

Imagine the surprise and horror of the guests in the banquet hall when the lips of the princess touched the first frog leg and the amphibian limb was transformed back to its princely human state.

John H. Dromey enjoys reading—mysteries especially—and writing in a variety of genres. He's had short fiction published in Alfred Hitchcock's Mystery Magazine, Crimson Streets, Stupefying Stories Showcase, and elsewhere, as well as in a number of anthologies, including Chilling Horror Short Stories (Flame Tree Publishing, 2015).

SURVIVAL

TIFFANY MICHELLE BROWN

The hatch screams as it opens, and I'm pulled toward darkness. My heart thrums. An errant tear flies from my cheek before it can stain my skin with salt. The expanse swirls in front of me. Greedy. Merciless. Perfect.

Teran shuttles across the room, shrieking, pawing at the cabin, but all within our ship is curved and slick. And he isn't affixed to the vessel with straps and magnets.

When he's swallowed up in pitch, I close the hatch and whisper, "Goodbye, brother."

A blade in hand, I seek out my mother, ready now, my resolve as vast as space.

Tiffany Michelle Brown is a native of Phoenix, Arizona, who ran away from the desert to live near sunny San Diego beaches. When she isn't writing, Tiffany can be found on a yoga mat, sipping whisky, or reading a comic book - sometimes all at once. Follow her adventures at tiffanymichellebrown.wordpress.com.

INSPIRATION POINT

DAVID BERNARD

"I don't normally do that on a first date," she lied, cuddling in the backseat of the car.

He smiled, continuing to trace her jaw line with small kisses that made her wish she hadn't already gotten dressed again.

He played with her hair. "Well, I don't normally pick up girls at high school dances either — especially when I'm supposed to be recruiting new members."

She sighed contently and began to rub his thigh. "Recruiting? Are you a religious kook or a political hack?"

He paused kissing her neck. "Neither, really" he murmured, and buried his teeth into her throat.

David Bernard is a native New Englander who lives in South Florida, albeit under protest. His previous works include short stories in anthologies such as Snowbound with Zombies (Post Mortem Press), Legacy of the Reanimator (Chaosium), and The Shadow over Deathlehem (Grinning Skull Press).

WELCOME TO EARTH

JENNIFER MOORE

We come in peace, they lisped, lulling us into a false sense of security with their round childlike eyes and empty silken lips. Peace. That's what it sounded like, without teeth or tongues to give proper shape to their words.

We lowered our guns, welcoming them to the planet.

Only it turned out it wasn't peace they'd come in after all. It was pieces. The poisonous, pulsing body sacs came next, venom squirting from every pore. Then the whipping laser-tails, barbed tongues and razored fangs.

Surrender or die, they snarled, their voices loud and clear now, even over the screaming.

Jennifer Moore is a British freelance writer and children's author. Her fiction has appeared in numerous publications on both sides of the Atlantic, including The Guardian, Mslexia, Daily Science Fiction, The First Line and Short Fiction. She is a previous winner of the Commonwealth Short Story Competition.

THE PICKUP

MICHAEL CARTER

I wake each night from the same dream. A man stands in my front yard staring back at me. Sometimes his face is distorted. Usually, it's aged and sad. He seems familiar.

When I wake this last time, I investigate. I walk to where the man stands and wait. Nothing.

Before I head back in, a delivery truck turns the corner onto my street. Perhaps it's him?

The truck doesn't stop, yet. As it passes, I see my reflection in the truck windows staring back with a big grin, even though I'm not smiling. And something is standing behind me.

Michael Carter is a short fiction and creative nonfiction writer who grew up reading an odd combination of sci-fi and Louis L'Amour books. He's also a ghostwriter in the legal profession and a Space Camp alum. He's online at www.michaelcarter.ink and @mcmichaelcarter.

DR. ALBIE

I. E. KNEVERDAY

It's not easy being the offspring of famed biologist Dr. Albie.

Never living up to his expectations.

Always lurking in his shadow.

And then there are the beatings. And the cold nights (like this one) that I must spend alone in the cellar, while Father is away giving lectures.

He hates when I use the F-word, mind you, preferring instead that I call him "Creator." (He told me as much one night while securing my chains.)

Like I said before, it's not easy being the offspring of famed biologist Dr. Albie.

But despite Father's monstrous ego, I still love him.

I. E. Kneverday is a writer of speculative fiction (including horror, sci-fi, & fantasy). His first book, The Woburn Chronicles: A Trio of Supernatural Tales Set in New England's Most Mysterious City, is available now. You can find more of his microfiction on Medium and at Kneverday.com.

THE TRUNK

TAMOHA SENGUPTA

Jahnvi walked toward the unused well. There was a trunk lying on the ground, and that was where the cries were coming from. Someone had put a baby inside? Horrified, she lifted the lid. And then she was falling...

The next thing she knew, she was inside the well— with just a circle of night sky visible above. As the clouds shifted, she saw what she was sitting on. A dead baby. She opened her mouth to scream. But nothing came out.

And then a faint sound reached her ears. Her voice— not the baby's— was now screaming for help.

Tamoha Sengupta lives in India. Her fiction has appeared in Daily Science Fiction, Zetetic: A Record of Unusual Inquiry, Fantastic Stories of the Imagination and elsewhere. She tweets @sengupta_tamoha.

GHOSTS OF THE PAST

WILL SHADBOLT

Finding ghosts wasn't hard--they congregated at their old ruins--killing them was where the difficulty lay. But that was why it made for such good sport.

I spotted a tall man near a forlorn structure and was quickly upon him.

He fought but was no match for my fists. Soon I had him pinned.

I eyed his pale skin: he'd make a good trophy.

"Please, let me go," he cried. "You used to be like me!" He clawed at my pink skin and third arm.

"That was then," I said, "and now you're just a ghost of the past."

Will has worked overseas in China as an English teacher and is currently a professional proofreader based near New York City. He has a story forthcoming in The Grievous Angel.

SOMETHING

KIM PLASKET

"I want to feel your pain" I hissed at him watching as he lay on the bed. The only part of him that could move was his eyes. I wanted to see pain, the only thing was hatred.

"So you hate me now" I cooed as I held the knife to his chest. "You told me I had your heart did you lie?"

"Blink once for yes. We cannot have a misunderstanding now"

He blinked just one time, tears falling from his eyes. "I will have to take it"

"We could have been something " sadly I smiled. "Now you die"

Kim Plasket is a Jersey girl at heart in sunny Florida. She has several short stories featured in anthologies such as 'Demonic Wildlife' and 'The Hunted', and Fireflies and Fairy dust she also has had a story featured in Shades of Santa with more to come.

CAROL ROSALIND SMITH

THE DEVIL WITHIN

From the moment my sibling was born I sensed the evil within. When they first brought him home I tried smothering him with a blanket. My parents thought I was playing peekaboo.

They thought it cute. They trusted me. Little did they realize.

While the household slept I scratched and pinched, jabbing at my brother's skin, sticking him with safety pins to ensure he would wake, priying his eyes open with my fingertips, searching for the flames of hell I was certain burnt deep inside.

Those liquid eyes told me all I needed to know. The devil always stared back.

Carol Rosalind Smith is an artist in the UK, combining poetry with art. Her words have been published by 101 words, Ellipsis Zine, Spelk Fiction, Visual Verse, Zeroflash, The Infernal Clock, Horror Tree's Trembling with Fear and in various anthologies. Twitter @carolrosalind
https://crsmith2016.wordpress.com.

LOVE AND HATE

R. G. HALSTEAD

Fire. Twelve-year-old Malcolm sure loved it. So far, he had burned down the grocery store, old Mr. Nordstrom's house and had just now returned from torching the school which he hated so much.

Getting underneath the covers of his bed, he muttered, "Got away with another one."

Malcolm closed his eyes and hugged his teddy bear. "It's not my fault, Mr. Fuzzy. My parents are real bad parents."

Sleep came to the boy.

His twin brother tied Malcolm to the bed. And set fire to it with the help of some gasoline.

"Let's see how you love this fire ..."

R. G. Halstead is a 62-year-old takes to writing late in his life.

MIDNIGHT IMPOSTER

JADE SWANN

"Mommy, I had a nightmare. Can I stay with you?"

"Sure, sweetie," Norma mumbled, half-asleep. The mattress bowed as Alice settled into bed. Norma vaguely registered the fur of Alice's teddy bear brushing up against her back before falling asleep.

KNOCK. KNOCK.

Norma startled awake.

"Mommy?" Alice called, her voice muffled by wood.

Norma rolled over with a yawn. "Come back to bed, sweetie."

"I can't. The door's locked."

Norma's eyes shot open. Two black holes stared back at her in the darkness, the gouged sockets empty and lifeless. A furry hand locked around her throat, cutting off her screams.

Jade Swann can be found writing with a cup of coffee in one hand and a Boston Terrier by her side. Her work has been published in Microfiction Monday Magazine, Every Day Fiction, and in the anthology Nonsensically Challenged: Volume 2.

THE FUTURE CONQUERERS

CHRISTINA SNG

"Once upon a time, we took over every living planet and sucked the life out of every creature we found. Surely there was one that could defeat us, but there were none. And so we lived happily ever after, on our Death Ships, cruising the Universe looking for more worlds to conquer and squelchy lives to kill. The end."

On the Death Ship, Mars Attacks, Prunella Oak tucks the children to bed with this story before their hibernation cycle. They beam and click their delight with their tiny pincers, soon dreaming of their future as war-mongering conquerers. Imprinting complete.

Christina Sng is the Bram Stoker Award®-winning author of A COLLECTION OF NIGHTMARES and Elgin Award nominees, ASTROPOETRY and AN ASSORTMENT OF SKY THINGS. Her fiction has appeared in Fantastic Stories of the Imagination, Grievous Angel, New Myths, and Space and Time. Visit her at http://www.christinasng.com.

SIX MORE WEEKS OF WINTER

TIANNA GROSCH

Persephone dug her fingernails into the earth and wiggled her hips trying to break free. The heat of the Underworld burned her ankles and the backs of her thighs – she knew any moment Hades would reclaim her.

Above, the grass was covered in frost, her mother's final grip in mourning.

Persephone could feel the sunshine warm on her neck, beginning to melt frost into dew.

Flames licked up her legs, tasting her skin as a hand reached up to anchor her below.

No matter how many times she attempted escape, she would always belong to the Underworld and its king.

Tianna Grosch is working on a debut novel in the woodlands of PA and received her MFA from Arcadia University. Her work has previously appeared or is forthcoming in EllipsisZine, Who Writes Short Shorts, New Pop Lit, Crack the Spine and others. Follow her @tiannag92. tiannag2412.wixsite.com/creativet

ALIEN AUTOPSY (CASE NOTES, ANCIENT ENGLISH TRANSLATION)

EZEKIEL KINCAID

The year was 9090. As with any new alien we've discovered, I examined the language first. The markings on the spacesuit seemed archaic, like nothing I'd seen before. The body laid naked on my table. It had grotesque smooth, skin covering its core and four tendrils. The two lower tendrils were larger. The other two came out from its side. At the end of each of those tendrils several smaller tendrils protruded. On the top of the core there were many tentacles and other odd structures. I glanced at the file for more information. TYPE: HUMAN. ORIGIN: EARTH. EXTINCT: 2525

Ezekiel Kincaid resides in Baton Rouge, Louisiana. For fun, he likes to train in martial arts and watch people get in socially awkward situation. The only other language he is fluent in is sarcasm. Zeke hates cat videos but loves watching wrestling promos from the 80's.

ON A WING AND A PRAYER

DOUGLAS PRINCE

Magic is a powerful thing.

The wind tore at Jamie's cheeks as he soared through the air, pyjama-clad legs clasped around the neck of the mighty dragon. He screamed in delight

as it banked and dived, miles above the crowded streets.

This is insane, he thought. This can't be happening.

Magic is a curious thing.

The wind tore at Jamie's cheeks as he plummeted through the air, pyjama-clad legs clasped around nothing at all. He screamed in terror as he tumbled over and over, miles above the crowded streets.

Magic is a powerful thing.

It has no time for non-believers.

Douglas Prince is a 28-year-old writer of horror and other dark fiction. Born in Melrose, Scotland, he now lives on the Wirral peninsula, in Merseyside, where he writes stories and reads more books than can possibly be good for him.

IT KNOCKED

SCOTT HUGHES

Duane answered the door and cussed. I heard a wet crack, then a flump.

It came into my room. I couldn't see good in the TV light. Some kinda giant crawdad walking upright. It climbed on me. I screamed and slapped at it. It stuck my belly, then ran off.

I'm 600 pounds, stuck in bed, so I cain't reach the phone or see about Duane. Hollering's useless. We don't live near nobody.

Whatever it put in me started eating my fat. It tickled. My stomach deflated. Now they're burrowing deeper, gnawing my insides. Damn, there's so many of them.

Scott Hughes's fiction, poetry, and essays have appeared in Crazyhorse, One Sentence Poems, Entropy, Deep Magic, Carbon Culture Review, Redivider, Redheaded Stepchild, PopMatters, Strange Horizons, Chantwood Magazine, Odd Tales of Wonder, The Haunted Traveler, Exquisite Corpse, Pure Slush, Word Riot, and Compaso: Journal of Comparative Research in Anthropology and Sociology. For more information, visit writescott.com.

THE THIRST OF WAR

JONATHAN FICKE

The incessant percussion of artillery fire laid the beat to my song of death. I danced in the lungs of the dying in the trenches of Ypres. In Passchendaele, I tap danced as the mud and the blood swallowed soul after damned soul. My spirit gripped old men in London and Paris and Berlin, and drove them to sacrifice the young to my insatiable thirst. The world went mad and a generation died. When nations, young and old, came together to halt the killing, I did not weep, I merely waited. My time would come again, and again, and again.

Jonathan Ficke lives outside of Milwaukee with his beautiful wife. His fiction has appeared in "Writers of the Future, Vol. 34" and "Tales of Ruma," and he muses online at jonficke.com and tweets (mostly about writing, basketball, and woodworking) @jonficke.

DEATH RUSH

C. COOCH

He glared at me out of eyeless sockets, his face full of dust and deep crevasses.

His gaze drifted by and he slinked over to the young girl. His long stick-like finger prodded her. I sensed the small soul diminishing; I closed my eyes as the rush I got peaked into a state of euphoria. Through doped up eyes I watched the silhouette of long cloak and scythe disappear. The girl's body remained in a pool of blood, where I'd left her.

I lobbed the bloodied knife into the murky canal.

I want his job, maybe next time I'll ask.

C. Cooch currently resides in Devon, UK. Married, with three dogs. Some thirty-odd years ago a teacher said the line "Oh if you were to just write stories instead of daydreaming.", and that is exactly what has been happening ever since.

SELF-DESTRUCTION BY STEEL

GABRIELLE BLEU

She claimed the cursed sword, but she misunderstood the wise woman's warning. Wielding the sword made her impervious to harm in battle, yes. She strode across the battlefield, blades bending from her body, arrows whistling around her. And the sword was a stealer of souls, yes, but not her enemies'. With each cut to a foe, each stab through a belly, each hack to an arm, a piece of her soul siphoned through the sword, and into the fatal wound.

She stood alone, triumphant, and empty. The field was strewn with bodies. She clutched her heart, and watched herself die.

Gabrielle Bleu's deepest fears are dogs and the ocean. She has been known, at various times, to swing around swords of varying sizes. She can be followed on Twitter @BeteMonstrueuse for her thoughts on bats, monsters, and old things buried in archives.

THE SMELL

JACK WOLFE FROST

That smell again. Musty, rotten, mouldy. I've known this many times. I'm blind, cannot move, but I feel rough ground beneath. I hear only the wind, it is the wind which blows at times the smell. I have no idea where I am, or who I am. Perhaps I am dead, and this is it.

I am hungry though. Death cannot be hunger? I try again to move an arm. This time, it twitches. Again. It becomes free.

I search my body. Where a leg is, my hand finds maggots, they crawl by the score.

The smell - food, at last.

Jack Wolfe Frost born in a storm in 1956, started writing dark works 35 years ago. He lives in a dark valley in the mountains of Wales, still writing dark stories. When not writing, he builds his shelter, and stocks with food and water, awaiting the apocalypse.

A LONELY ROAD

DENZELL COOPER

I met her on a lonely road, face paler than the silver moonlight, eyes like dark holes.

"Do you know the way?" She asked. An owl shrieked. The wind rustled the trees.

A shiver rocked my body. I tried not to look into her face. "Where are you going?" My voice trembled, but not from the cold.

"Not me," she said. "No, not me."

"Sorry." I shook my head, my voice barely a whisper. "I have to get home. My husband, you see. My baby..." I turned, heels tick-tocking.

Headlights. An engine.

Her voice behind. "Do you know the way?"

Denzell Cooper is a multi-genre writer from Cornwall, England. He's a keen amateur ghost hunter who has walked many lonely roads looking for evidence of the departed. Find him online at his blog, www.denofhorror.co.uk, or on Twitter @DenzellCooper.

FOR SALE IN MYANMAR

LINDY GREAVES

I squat in the dirt. The girls either side of me don't speak. Just the men. Short spiky syllables I don't understand. The sun sears through palm leaves throwing knife-shaped shade across my skin. I scrunch my eyes. When everything is dark there is no shadow.

Suddenly, a word I recognise.

Dollar.

I picture its round shape pushing out Father's lips and rolling off his tongue before he sold me to the scorpion-tattoo man. That was yesterday. He didn't get any. Only a wad of new kyat disappearing into his fist. Didn't even look back.

I squat in the dirt.

Lindy Greaves has ghostwritten as a career criminal and a missionary nun. She lives in the Midlands, England with her husband and kids, writing articles, stories and tinkering with her novel.

THE JEALOUS WISH

SHAWN KLIMEK

I wish I had been more lovable.

When Emmett returned, it was not to keep his promises, but to introduce his beautiful new fiancé, Nora. Despite my jealousy, she was difficult to hate; their love made my own feel cheap. There is a wishing well on the outskirts of town where, for centuries, every bride has gone on the eve of her wedding, to wish for a happy marriage. To prove to Emmett that I could be a bigger person, I showed Nora where it was. The well is deep and the overlook narrow. The bigger person has an advantage.

Shawn Klimek writes fiction and poetry to entertain. More of his flash fiction can be found in CafeLit and his poetry on NewMyths.com. /@shawnmklimekauthor.

NOT WORRIED

DIANE ARRELLE

Originally Published in The Drabbler

I asked, as a joke, right before I said, I do, "Does her kind eat their mates?"

"Nah," Matheson said smiling, "but you gotta be really careful when they're pregnant."

Now my wife's with child, but I'm not worried.

Matheson's wife's pregnant too and in her nesting stage, and Matheson's gone, vanished. She decorated their nursery and I couldn't help but notice Matheson's fairy tattoo, the one he had done of his wife, glued to the wall over the crib.

But I'm not worried. Although my wife's been sharpening the kitchen knives as she gets closer to her due date.

Diane Arrelle, the pen name of South Jersey writer Dina Leacock, has sold more than 250 short stories and has two published books. Her third book, Seasons On The dark Side, will be available in May 2018. Recently retired from being director of a senior center, she is co-owner of Jersey Pines Ink LLC. She resides with her husband and new cat on the edge of the Pine Barrens (home of the Jersey Devil).

SKIN AND BONE

ELIZABETH DEARBORN

Originally Published in Flashshot

I saw ghosted images of the alien inside Joanna. It was ordained that I, who loved her more than life, would cut it away.

She lay unconscious and naked before me. I sliced her from side to side. Blood spurted from the wound, but she slept on.

I reached inside her with bloody hands and cut the monster out. A malformed sphere, covered with skin and bits of bone.

We had so hoped for another child, but it was not to be.

As my acolyte sewed my wife back together, I flipped the switch.

"Dr. Stewart dictating a dermoid cystectomy ..."

———

Elizabeth writes short fiction and computer code. She worked in pathology for several years and is now retired.

A SMALL MISUNDERSTANDING

DIANE ARRELLE

Originally Published in The Special Drabbler 2

I was a sure bet to win the Intergalactic Culinary Prize! Instead, I'm disqualified and under arrest.

I was competing with the Earthlady. We were locked in a kitchen for 5 hours with 10 ingredients from each the other's planet and told "make it homestyle."

The lady, looking unhappy, mixed things together that a five-year-old knew spelled disaster. Me, I sat for three hours puzzling over the strange array of foods. Then it hit me, fried chicken, an Earth delicacy!

It looked great, the drumstick tasted just like chicken. Seriously, how was I to know human limbs don't grow back?

Diane Arrelle, the pen name of South Jersey writer Dina Leacock, has sold more than 250 short stories and has two published books. Her third book, Seasons On The dark Side, will be available in May 2018. Recently retired from being director of a senior center, she is co-owner of Jersey Pines Ink LLC. She resides with her husband and new cat on the edge of the Pine Barrens (home of the Jersey Devil).

SATURN'S FINAL ROTATION

TIANNA GROSCH

When you're the only man living in space, you worry about space mites. Things people on Earth never worry about.

The mites attack when Saturn makes its final rotation for the third day or is it night? Time shifts when you live up here. My suit does nothing to protect me, they chew through the fabric and burrow inside me. I have so many space mites living inside, I must glow like a lanternfish, a beam of light.

Can they see me glowing from Earth?

I have half a mind to remove my helmet for a breath of fresh air.

Tianna Grosch is working on a debut novel in the woodlands of PA and received her MFA from Arcadia University. Her work has previously appeared or is forthcoming in EllipsisZine, Who Writes Short Shorts, New Pop Lit, Crack the Spine and others. Follow her @tiannag92. tiannag2412.wixsite.-com/creativet.

THE ROAD WARRIOR

ERICKA KAHLER

The front quarter panel crushed my legs as a blond woman knelt next to me. "Shhhhhh," she said. Her knee rattled my license plate. CATCH ME - a perpetual challenge to anyone in my rear view mirror. No one had, until now.

She looked down at the plate. "You shouldn't have tempted Fate that way," she said. "She's kind of a bitch."

I felt a jolt when her hands rested on my chest. I fluttered my fingers. My heart fluttered still with them. "What are you doing to me?"

She smiled. "Taking you to Valhalla. Fate gave me a heads up."

Ericka Kahler has lived in eight states, each progressively further north. Her short fiction has appeared in dark fantasy anthologies and the odd horror magazine. Her creative non-fiction has appeared in Chicken Soup for the Soul and literary journals. You can find her website at http://erickakahler.wordpress.com/.

BLOOD WILL OUT

JAN KANEEN

Abandoned attics stale and still, decades of dust making ghosts of everything.

Undisturbed.

Dust upon dust muffling the hubbub below, stifling the thrum of those living beneath, lifetimes away

They keep to the shadows, out of the white light that sometimes struggles through dirty windows, but tonight is different.

Midsummer midnight. Full blood moon. Rising.

Lucifer's twilight falls slant into faded places, drawing them up in their millions.

Italic mots, sparse at first, rising in thin swirls lighter than night, becoming bone and flesh, coagulating into skinless limbs and twisted faces, dripping claret. Embodied at last, to drink their fill.

Jan Kaneen is a self-identifying weirdo who writes brief fiction from her cottage in the Cambridgeshire fens. She's been published round and about, and won comps at Molotov Cocktail, Horror Scribes and Zero Flash. She's finishing an MA in Creative Writing at the OU and was nominated for a 2018 Pushcart and Best on the Net. She blogs at https://jankaneen.com/ and tweets as @Jankaneen1.

SUNLIGHT

ADITYA DESHMUKH

I remember the touch of sunlight. Once it soothed me. Once I saw elysian dreams in its warmth. But now, when it falls on my skin, it burns. Those dreams are long dead, and sunlight is merely now something from the past that haunts my present, torturing me by showing glimpses of a heaven I could've had.

The madness of my twisted desires grows, my heart craves for sin, and the bloodlust of my soul is much stronger than ever before. I'm turning into darkness, and soon I'll be unstoppable. For no light can vanquish the monster I'd have become.

Aditya is an emerging writer and has been published by Clarendon Publications recently in a flash fiction anthology that was an Amazon bestseller in France and Canada.

GRAVE ERROR

KIM PLASKET

Darkness falls, I lay near where you are. I tell you all the things you want to hear. I tell you how I adore you, how you are the only one I will ever love.

You told me how I never could measure up. How just one time you wished I would do what you told me.

I wonder how cold you are now lying in your grave. Just this one time, you should have kept your mouth closed. I had the gun to kill myself but you said I should just kill you.

So I did willingly.

Kim Plasket is a Jersey girl at heart in sunny Florida. She has several short stories featured in anthologies such as 'Demonic Wildlife' and 'The Hunted', and Fireflies and Fairy dust she also has had a story featured in Shades of Santa with more to come.

A TIME AND A PLACE

DOUGLAS PRINCE

Graham Vaughn III was no academic, but he was a genius.

You've likely seen his face in the Museum of Future Past, a silent scream carved in relief from the granite of his Montana homeland.

A work of art? Not quite.

More a quirk of science.

Vaughn's maiden voyage was 100% successful. He travelled 185 million years

back in time, and didn't move an inch in space.

It was Montana when he left, the supercontinent of Laurasia when he arrived.

Imagine his surprise – and his terror – when he materialised...

...in the middle of a mountain, long since lost to history.

Douglas Prince is a 28-year-old writer of horror and other dark fiction. Born in Melrose, Scotland, he now lives on the Wirral peninsula, in Merseyside, where he writes stories and reads more books than can possibly be good for him.

PARASITE

SIMON PINKERTON

Nobody else can see it in you. You never pay it a moment's thought, except to think that it's something that maybe happens to other people—and then you have it. It spreads to everything, gets everywhere.

After a couple of months you're almost ready to give up. You would do anything to be somebody else. I stood there looking into my bloodshot, angry eyes in the splintered bathroom mirror that I had just cracked with the side of my fist, screaming at my reflection, imploring God-knows who for it not to be this alien, fractured, shameful face staring back.

Simon Pinkerton is from London, England, and is best pals with all the royals, including Royal Crown Cola, Crown Royal Whisky and the color Royal Blue. He writes fiction and humor and can be found on Twitter @simonpinkerton.

HEAD CASE

MIKE MURPHY

Kyle's head felt funny. He had been using it all morning, and it had gone kind of squishy. He touched it with his free hand. Definitely not okay.

He got out of the recliner and shuffled to the kitchen, bringing his head with him. He emptied the spent cigarette butts into the trash, but the hollowed-out skull of his latest victim still felt mushy. He plopped it into the barrel and got another one from the fridge.

A girl this time. He smiled. Kyle carried the new ashtray to the recliner, sat, and enjoyed a smoke with his lady friend.

Mike has had over 150 audio plays produced. He's won five Moondance awards.

His work has appeared in several magazines and anthologies. His script "The Candy Man" was produced as a short film under the title Dark Chocolate. He won the inaugural Marion Thauer Brown Audio Drama Scriptwriting Competition.

BLOOD TRANSFUSION

JOHN KUJAWSKI

Everyone was worried when they didn't hear from me. They came by and found me on the floor in the bathroom. I was literally starving to death.

Soon, I was brought to a medical facility and hooked up to some tubes. I received a blood transfusion because I was so frail and weak.

That was when I decided to make changes in my life. I soon recovered and starting taking better care of myself.

I found the perfect victim in an alley that I could feast on. After all, a vampire needs blood in order to have a healthy life.

John Kujawski has interests that range from guitars to the Incredible Hulk. He was born and raised in St. Louis, Missouri and still lives there to this day.

IRON WILL

JILLIAN BOST

Korina took a deep, steady breath. "I want my daughter back. Give her to me now, and nothing—no one—will be harmed."

She held back a wince as the jeers and hisses surrounded her, in the dry grass, the prickly bushes, and cold trees. "My daughter. Now."

"Go home, human," one of the faeries heckled. "She's ours now. You'll never see her again."

"One more chance," Korina said. "My daughter."

The forest erupted in laughter. Taunts followed Korina as she went back to her car. She popped the trunk, displaying the vast stores of iron inside.

"It's your funeral."

Jillian Bost is an avid reader, and occasionally writes, too. She's been published by Feed Your Monster, Fundead Publications, and The Flash Fiction Press. For more on her writing and other random things, follow her on Twitter at @JillianBost.

HUMAN IN ANY OTHER FORM

TIANNA GROSCH

Each morning, she watches the tawny, ragged fox cross her trimmed lawn where trees claim the earth and fog wraps trunks like beckoning fingers, shrouding oaks in mystery.

His black-tipped paws barely brush the earth as he weaves like a needle and thread, effortless on his journey despite the unnatural, crooked arch of his back and his hair spotty with bald spots.

The vibrant red radiates like fire among the forest, teasing her eye.

He looks in her direction and she can see, he's not a fox at all.

His eyes are very human.

His lips curl in a smile.

Tianna Grosch is working on a debut novel in the woodlands of PA and received her MFA from Arcadia University. Her work has previously appeared or is forthcoming in EllipsisZine, Who Writes Short Shorts, New Pop Lit, Crack the Spine and others. Follow her @tiannag92. tiannag2412.wixsite.-com/creativet.

IT'S A LIVING

PATRICK CROSSEN

It's a living, but grave robbing is lousy work at the best of times. At the lousiest of times, it's shit. Still, with each inch that my spade sunk into the wet October earth, I never considered stopping.

A voice called out and I slid into the grave as the guard swept through. He'd pass along and I'd continue.

A light blinded me.

When he lowered his flashlight, I saw him standing over me. He picked up my shovel and began to throw the dirt back in. I suppose that's how he kept attendance up. For him, it's a living.

Patrick Crossen is a creative writing major in Pittsburgh, PA. When he's not checking his mailbox for his Hogwarts letter, he spends his time writing sketch comedy, film reviews, and creating his own magical worlds.

COUNTING CORPSES

KARL EL-KOURA

Two old men drive around a battlefield, loading bodies into their trucks. The war has been so devastating that counting corpses is the only way to declare a winner.

"Young people," the northern man snorts, as they sort through the next pile. "You don't live to our age by shooting each other."

"You can say that again, brother," the southern man says.

The sun sets well before they're done.

"How many?" the southern man says

"Seventy-six. You?"

"Also seventy-six." It was one less than that, but the southern man pulls out a gun and adds another point to his side.

Karl El-Koura was born in Dubai, United Arab Emirates and now resides in Canada's capital city with his beautiful editor-wife and their adorable tiny human. Almost seventy of Karl's short stories and articles have been published in magazines since 1998. To find out more, visit Karl's website at www.ootersplace.com.

NO RAPTURE

MIKKO RAUHALA

Julia studied the papers spread out in front of her and frowned. Then she addressed the group of survivors: "Poll results are in. Our commonality is that we're all atheists here. All the religious folk are dead."

Richard looked pensive. "This was no rapture, though, what with the exploding heads. It's as if there actually is a god, but he's gotten sick of believers."

Suddenly, his eyes went wide. "Oh shi-" he managed before his brains decorated the wall.

There were gasps and shocked looks all around. Then the rest of the heads started to pop in order of quick-wittedness.

Mikko Rauhala is a speculative fiction writer from Finland. His English debut short story, The Guardian of Kobayashi, was published in the Never Stop anthology at Worldcon 75. His drabbles and other flash stories may be found in The Self-Inflicted Relative anthology and on 101words.org.

TECHITIS

MADDY HAMLEY

Ever since the first glint of green enamel, gradually seeping across the surface of the chip, we knew it would be trouble. We instituted quarantines, decontamination and sterilisation protocols. But we weren't dealing with biology. The disease spread, bringing down chips, processors, servers.

The populace was no help. It fought to preserve the glinting emerald crusts in elaborate shrines. Infested hard-drives and phones glittered from the corners of every living room.

It was only a matter of time, then, until the first pathologist produced a glinting green pacemaker, and amputees screamed as they lost their arms and legs once more.

Maddy Hamley's work has appeared on Paragraph Planet and in Sensorially Challenged Vol. 1. Currently suspended in the space between jobs and cities, she spends far too much time writing Twitter fiction as @nossorgs and occasionally cursing at untranslatable Bavarian proverbs in her capacity as a bilingual translator.

BLOOD RAIN

TAMLYN DREAVER

The blood rain came in the first month of the new year. People grew used to the fat red droplets of water. The streets looked like murder scenes with their puddles, and pools, dams, and rivers seemed to flow black.

Some blamed mining, and others the explosion of the international space station. Tests came up clean, bottled water ran low, and there was no choice but to drink it.

When blood-red slugs burst from tanks and pipes and dams – and from people who'd drunk the water – there wasn't enough organisation left to name it what it was: an alien invasion.

Tamlyn Dreaver grew up in rural Western Australia, spent eight years in Melbourne, and is now back in Perth. She's never had a secret basement or a dragon nesting in the backyard so she writes stories about them instead.

She can be found at www.tamlyndreaver.com and tweeting at @tamlyn_-dreaver.

LUCI

CHRISTINA SNG

"How could you not know he was the devil?" Mother screamed as she stared furiously at my rapidly growing belly.

"He was handsome and he had a halo..." I spluttered, but it was no use. My folly had always been pretty boys.

The baby arrived with horns as expected. Mother put it in the nursery with the rest of my babies.

"No more fraternizing with Lucifer or you'll be banished from Heaven forever!"

I lowered my head and tried to look remorseful.

Luci promised he would be back. He wanted lots of mini-hims and mini-mes, enough to form an army.

———

Christina Sng is the Bram Stoker Award®-winning author of A COLLECTION OF NIGHTMARES and Elgin Award nominees, ASTROPOETRY and AN ASSORTMENT OF SKY THINGS. Her fiction has appeared in Fantastic Stories of the Imagination, Grievous Angel, New Myths, and Space and Time. Visit her at http://www.christinasng.com.

WHAT ALICE WANTS

DAVID RAE

You called again. "I miss you." Well, I miss you too.

I think back to that time. I imagine your laughter. I should have held you forever. I should have been stronger. I smell the roses in the night air.

Alice sneered, "How cliché; with an au pair."

So angry; couldn't she understand.

Once you were gone, there was no more talk of divorce.

Every night you call.

I miss you too, but I am so weak.

Alice is shouting from the house; what does she want now. I push the earth back and put the spade in the shed.

David lives in Scotland. He loves stories that exist just below the surface of things, like deep water. He has most recently had work published or forthcoming in; THE FLATBUSH REVIEW, THE HORROR TREE, LOCUST, ROSETTA MALEFICARIUM, SHORT TALE 100 and 50 WORD STORIES. You can read more at Davidrae-stories.com.

THE ANNUAL VISIT

CLIO NIMA

Originally Published in Bete Noire Magazine

Once a year, on Easter's Eve, my grandma pays a visit. I calm her hair and arrange the flowers she brings. Nowadays, the time seems to have stopped, yet we talk about the weather and the people around us. Before the night falls, she knows everyone's tidings. How young Lily broke a bone, how Miss Fiona's flowers perished, how the Chans dropped their jaw when the priest came by. I really love her visits; she is the only one who sincerely listens. Then, she sends me a kiss goodbye, she lights the candle next to my tombstone and fares well.

Clio Nima comes from Greece. She studied business administration but dropped out before graduation then worked as a teacher for English as a foreign language for three years and now works in the tourism industry. She has also published a children's book in Greek. Reading and writing is what makes her world go 'round. She can be found at https://www.facebook.com/ClioNima/

THE PROGRAM

DENNY E. MARSHALL

Thomas wakes up in a dark room. The walls and ceiling look like stainless steel.

Thomas looks around causing a light to go on.

A door opens and someone walks in. More lights go on, the walls and ceiling change color.

"Hello Thomas how are you feeling? My name is Ruth." Said Ruth.

"Where am I? Why am I not in Tacoma? Where are my friends? " Asks Thomas.

"You where in a coma. There's no such thing as Tacoma, or Earth for that matter. Earth is just a program the federation uses for people in a coma." Said Ruth.

Denny E. Marshall has had art, poetry, and fiction published. One recent credit is fiction in Night To Dawn 33 April 2018. See more at www.dennymarshall.com.

I SLEW THE BLACKWING

JOACHIM HEIJNDERMANS

They said it couldn't be done. That I'd fall for its trap. But look at me now. Blood on my blade. Broken scales scattered across the cavern floor. Its tongue dangling limp from its mouth. I did it. I slew the Blackwing.

They warned me before I left. That the moment our eyes met, I'd be trapped in its dreamsnare, locked in a fugue state with visions of my greatest desires. Forever dreaming, 'till the last beat of my heart, while the beast laughs.

They were fools. I did the impossible. I slew the Blackwing and emerged victorious.

Didn't I?

Joachim Heijndermans is a writer and artist from the Netherlands. He's been published in a number of science fiction and fantasy magazines, such as Asymmetry Fiction, Metaphorosis and Mad Scientist Journal. In his spare times he paints, read and collects toys.

VIRGIL'S LOAD

DAN ALLEN

Running face sickness took Makawee down shortly after the twins were birthed. Virgil made do best he could, cookin' an' scrubbin', but he wasn't meant to be no mother. He taught them boys to chore soon as they could walk, but still, Virgil carried too heavy a load. He took them boys on hiatus to the top of Lookout Ridge and they stood each a side of him, tall and proud, leaning over the edge. Far below the prairie dust carried whispers of advice. Virgil put a hand on one back and, with the slightest pressure, he made his choice.

Dan was selected into the HWA Mentorship program and had the privilege of working with JG Flaherty. Dan's work appears in "Secret Stairs: A tribute to Urban Legend" from Silver Empire. He has also been featured in Dark Dossier's Halloween 2017, Jitter Press, Horrified Press, and Celenic Earth Publications. Visit Dan at www.danallenhorror.com

AFTERWORD

I hope you've enjoyed this short anthology of dark drabbles. Reviews are important to any book's success and if you feel so inclined, please leave a review of your thoughts and feelings of this anthology on Goodreads, Amazon, Audible, Barnes and Noble, and anywhere else reviews are read to encourage or discourage others. Thanks again for reading Drabbledark, I leave you with one final drabble from Robert Dawson.

Mortwood Abbey
Robert Dawson
Originally Published in SpeckLit

"I don't like this, Lanceton." Dr. James tried to look away from the grotesque statue, but the recently discovered crypt under the ruins of Mortwood Abbey was otherwise empty. His eye, finding no resting place in the gloom, was drawn back to the dreadful thing.

"Superstitious?"

"No. Just prudent."

"Hmmph! Say, you're the classicist here. Be a good chap and translate that inscription?"

" 'CUM INSCII CENTUM FABULAS CENTUM VERBORUM SCRIBERINT REDEBO.' James hardly hesitated. 'I shall return when the unknowing have written a hundred hundred-word stories.'"

"Mad! Whoever heard of hundred-word stories?"

There was a grating, scraping sound behind them.

KICKSTARTER SUPPORTERS

A special shout out goes to the following people for helping bring this project to life through out Kickstarter campaign. Thank you. We couldn't have done it without you!

Nicholas Diak

David Ballard

Jharper

Doctor Impossible

Rachel Kelley

Stewie

Steve Arensberg

David Queen

Aaron Turko

MoistVomit

Cato Vandrare

Guthrie Taylor

David Rae

David Jeremy Ducey

Jefferson Mills

Thomas

Dickon Springate

Aly Rhodes

Dagmar

Heather

Antoinettemarie Kalmus

Edmund Schluessel
Matt Miller
Tiff Reynolds
Tianna Grosch
JT Grosch
Joseph
David
Benjamin Widmer
Software Bloke
Valeria Ballerini

Made in the USA
Coppell, TX
12 January 2020

14428060R00065